www.tredition.de

AF202335

At the Edge of Life
and Other Stories

Essa Bayoumi

www.tredition.de

Verlag und Druck:
tredition GmbH, Halenreie 40-44, 22359 Hamburg

ISBN
Paperback: 978-3-347-28690-0
Hardcover: 978-3-347-28691-7
e-Book: 978-3-347-28692-4

Dedication

to my wife Renate Westphal-Bayoumi

Prologue

I wrote these short stories in a long span of time and a large distance of space. The time stretches as long as three decades and, the distance extends between my home country Egypt and my now living country Germany. Here I must say that Time and Space have different meaning and effect for the writer than for a normal person, who he occasionally is.

Time for a writer – at least for me – has no direction, except the way I look at life and those who miraculously feel it. Space for me is where nature shows its marvel and guides us to engage with it. Therefore, the sequence of the fifteen stories contained in this collection does not follow the direction of time familiar to us: past towards future. Nor it follows location of places: south to north. But it has though a hidden thread that the reader can detect if she, or he, positioned herself, or himself, at the edge of life. At that edge, Man forgets certain time and specific place, and gets a glimpse of the eternal world inside himself. Or, that is at least what I hoped for.

I wrote these stories two times; one time in Arabic language, my mother tongue, which were published in one book in Egypt in 2019, and some of them were already published in Al Jassra magazine in Doha, Qatar. And one time in English for my friends who were interested in my literature but unable to read them in Arabic. It was the advice of my wife to try to share them with a wider range of English readers or those who are interested in a glimpse at the edge of life where we all can meet and become friends.

Essa Bayoumi, Hamburg, Germany, 16th February, 2021

Contents

1.   At the Edge of Life

It started as a sunny day of June. It happened in Schwedt, a north-eastern town in Germany. On the border line between Germany and Poland the River Oder flows freely and comfortably, till it meets the Baltic Sea. On that river; Schwedt is located, a rather small but truly magnificent town of nature. Was it a geographical edge that created two different cultures? Or was it a different manifestation of the power of life?

He started from Garten Street, taking the direction to the river side through Berliner Street. The beauty of the town was unfolding to him with each step. The flowers with glowing colors of red, violet and white were distributed all along. Both sides of the road were surrounded by the rich greenness of the thick and tall trees until the blueness of the water, stretched in front of him, started confessing the glory of the river.

The pleasant smell of the air, he breathed, was mixed with quietness he never felt before. He selected a bench out of many and sat; sinking in a world he created, at the edge between reality and fantasy. The sky expressed full agreement with his view.

Individual Baltic seagulls were flying around him or riding the water surface next to a group of swimming ducks. Each one was minding its own interest, and he tried to do that too. He opened his book where he stopped and resumed reading. He felt belonging to the same world. It was a book about Life on the Edge.

-2-

One hour passed while he was fascinating his mind with quantum definition of biological compass. The authors Jim Al-Khalili and John-joe McFadden were trying to explore how robins find their destination thousands of miles away whether at day or night over land or sea.

He noticed that all the chairs and benches around him were occupied by people; mostly elder couples enjoying the warmness and beauty of the day. That is except one lady who was already sitting on the other end of his bench. Maybe she preferred the river view from that side, where the sense of time was ignored.

He seemed so taken by his reading to notice her, taking her seat on his bench. She was in her fifties, wearing not much make up to conceal slight wrinkles around her tight lips and left eye. That was what a quick look to his right side interpreted. His instantaneous memory reflected her dark brown dress that did not fit her complexion; but probably her mood. A small black bag was laid next to her. Her eyes were fixed at the water surface.

After few minutes her hand raised to her face and wiped something off her eyes. Was she crying?

She was opening her bag when their eyes met. He felt embarrassed and quickly shifted his attention to his book when her voice reached him: "I am sorry to disturb you".

He felt the warmness of her voice communicated in the same moment through her eyes as an electron being found in two positions simultaneously; what quantum scientists call superposition. He also felt her sadness; trying to reach out despite her resistance to let it go.

"It is a lovely day, I am happy to share it with everyone, humans, birds, flowers..." he said.

Some seconds passed before she encouraged herself to say, "I forgot to water my flowers yesterday. In the mid of night, I recalled and became panicked they might die. I went out in the darkness and showered them with water. I am not sure they will survive. They are too delicate".

"Is that why you feel sad?" he could not stop himself from asking her.

Some minutes passed before her voice reached him again: "My husband died few days ago, the flowers are my life connection. Do you think they will survive?"

"Not only with water your connection to life survives", he said, while he looked to the many flowers beautifully surrounding the place. "Sadness comes from life not from death. How we feel sad for what we don't know?" he added.

"Death takes our hope. My husband lasted on the sick bed for years. With all the pain he suffered, there was still some hope. Now, there is no pain and no hope either." She spoke.

He was not prepared for such thoughts at that beautiful day, but the dark-colored clothes she was wearing gave him the warning. The lady seemed lonely and in despair to talk her feelings.

He tried to console her by saying," life is an individual task, look to this faraway swimming duck. It took its way across the river all alone".

"Maybe human race is the weakest of living forms except for the mind. The flowers, I forgot to attend, might perish but they will feel no sorrow", she reflected.

"Science is still unable to explain our consciousness which proves your point", he noted.

She seemed lost in her thoughts. Few more minutes passed in silence. He was holding his book to resume reading then her voice came penetrating his world once more.

She said," I spent very good years with Hans, we did everything we wanted to do as a couple. We travelled the world and had a good fun, until he got ill. That was not planned".

She was following a flying seagull with her eyes while the past was sadly flying in her consciousness.

"He was not a demanding patient and took it as part of his life deal. He believed that our existence is eternal although in constant change. I miss him already very much", she added.

The woman was really in agony despite her attempts to show self-control.

"The historian Yuval Noah Harari anticipated that Man will achieve immortality in the near future and becomes what he named Homo Deus; he means the Man who is his own God. Would that solve the problem? I think, death is part of the solution not part of a problem. Man does not accept the world he found himself in, and tries to be different although everything around him tells the same story once and again in many versions and limitless ways. We should learn from the ducks and seagulls, from every flower and tree; that we are not different." He said assuming she was not listening to him.

He was shocked when he heard her saying," If the death is part of the solution, then committing suicide is a way out".

"Have you seen ever a tree commits suicide or a duck drowns itself? We don't come to life by our own will, similarly our departure, as long as we keep consistency", he immediately responded.

Now, he felt they belong to two different worlds. He noticed a mobile ice-cream van just parked not far from where they sat. He put his book on the bench between them, and excused himself for a minute and headed towards the van. There was a bunch of kids already queued, so he stood waiting for his turn. After some minutes, he came back to where he left her, carrying two packs of nice ice cream. She was gone. His book "Life on the Edge" which he left on the bench has also disappeared.

-3-

He took his way back to "Andersen hotel" where he stayed. Without the book in his hand, he felt strange, like something was missing. The roads were almost empty while crowds of heavy clouds were gathering in the sky; a warning of rain. A sudden weather change was not unusual at that time of the year. He did not carry his umbrella but few more steps and he will be in his room.

He entered his room with a heavy mind that occupied his morning. In the room he found his wife waiting for him. She did not inform him of her coming. She even did not know where he stayed. His surprise was beyond explanation when he spotted his missing book on the table next to her.

2.   A Special Connection

It was dark, not only because of the approach of midnight, but also because of his mood. The moon was shielded by heavy clouds and by complete loneliness. At that spot to the Mediterranean coast, the sea waves were the single confirmation of continuous existence and dialogue.

For three hours, he was following each and every single change in his surrounding area, which at that point seemed challengingly constant. Maybe that is why he was here. His reflection on the nature was undeniable, or was it the other way around. At any case, with unity partners are equals. And that is where he likes to be.

"But you can't be always there". She responded to his description of his favorite place.

"Facing the truth for a lifetime is sort of punishment," he answered. "Only prophets are able to do so," he added.

He invited her to that place as a declaration of sincerity. She accepted his company not only curiously but with a sense of attraction and love to be a part of his life that might be uncovered to her. His or hers!

When they arrived, the beach was completely deserted. It is not usual to seek such universal vagueness in winter time when it is so cold, nor at that point of time where night befalls. He indicated a nearby rock as his permanent destination.

She whispered in a try not to disturb the compelling serenity that has taken her, "that place can hardly accommodate two persons."

He didn't seem like to respond to her comment while approaching the indicated spot, but he said when they reached there, "we are not two at the moment, here things are looked at differently, the place has its superiority."

She said, not without sadness, "here you don't need me or anybody else."

"The need for you is always there", he said looking into the endlessness.

They sat on the rock as far as it could get them, their thoughts drifting to unknown boundaries.

She said after a while, "why vast openness has such a magic effect on us, being a seaside or a desert?".

He responded, knowing her love for the desert, "is Man part of nature or apart from it? I think with such vast openness Man feels hope, the limitlessness frees his imagination against his fated physics."

She became pleased that her lurking feeling could be shared and so clearly expressed, " that is quite true. I never could understand people who are afraid of desert and feel helpless facing it. On the contrary, I always felt such hope, you have just defined, like I feel now looking into the sea. Thank you for inviting me to your special place."

After a long while he suddenly said, " I don't know why Man has always to look for someone to share his feelings and ideas with, that does not fit with nature where every creature stands alone for its fate. With someone around, the openness becomes less, unless he is not observed!"

She failed to reach him and said in disappointment, " is this a request to me to leave?"

He smiled inwardly and said, "if you weren't a part of the nature or a special part of my fate, I would not have asked you to come here."

She didn't like her being a part of his fate as he put it and said, "fate is something we are forced to accept, you are not forced to accept me."

He said in a true passion, "my dear, accepting fate is a way to choose it, that is what being in this place is all about. Haven't you agreed of its hope- creating power?"

She was lost in a deep thinking. When her head turned to his and the eyes met, she said in such divine simplicity, "I love you."

3.   Elbe River and the only possible truth

The weather in Hamburg that morning of September was especially uncertain. Although there was expectation of rain, a period of sunshine was equally forecasted. Would be there a wind; strong enough for a sailing boat to try a journey? The cloudy sky did not tell. The grey color dominates. Only the hope of change made it tolerable. It was time to go as it gets; except for those who put their will in front of nature regardless of the end results. Their deeds are their results.

He made up his mind and headed west to "Wedel", where "Hamburger Yachthafen" is located, where his sailing boat was docked. Today, he promised himself to find the truth.

After a night of doubts and uncertainties his life seemed a hard question to answer. Sailing will help, he was sure, not only to find an answer for a night's question, hard as it was, but for a whole life mystery. Or, so he thinks.

After decades of being together and with daughters and sons sitting around, his wife challenged him with the question: why he really lives, would be there a difference if his being stops to exist, does it really matter for her life to last with him?

It was obvious for him that a crisis was in the making and such questions were lurking in her mind originally, with herself being the subject of doubt; not him. He used to be the reason for any uncertainty faced her mind, and she used to obtain the answer that brings back her trust in life. But, not this time.

The children attendance to follow this was her message that a decision was made. The dilemma was that she was not asking the right questions, the confusion was her intention, not the clarity, the anarchy not the order. She had no intention for a truth to seek.

He entered the marina with heavy heart and preoccupied mind, why human being is destined to the misery of ignorance. He parked his car and walked the distance to where his boat was laid within hundreds of boats queued in parallel rows, waiting for those who seek a journey to the only possible truth. Is the Elbe capable to manage them all and provide each of them a destiny?

-2-

She was standing on board her small boat, located in the same row where his boat was, only few other boats in between. He recognized her silhouette while approaching, she seemed to be inspecting her boat's single sail, but nothing indicated her intention to start a journey. They were neighbors and members in the same yacht owners' association since years.

He noticed her smile upon recognition, before her voice welcomed him: "good morning Karl, you are not sailing today, are you?" She was in her forties, slim, short; her face speaks of joy, sharp eyes and body of energy.

"I want to give it a try, Doris, that is what remains", he said.

She noticed his distraction. He did not stop when he passed her to have a little chat as he usually did. Her voice reached him while he was getting closer to his boat, " are you sailing alone today, no one from the family joins you?"

"No one trusts the weather as I do", he replied stopping for a moment, considering what he was saying. "They think; for sailing you only need a good wind", he added.

"Probably today is not the best to try, if you seek a proper journey", she said.

For a moment he thought the conversation was meaningless, nevertheless he said, "every day is proper for sailing, you only need to seek the truth".

He did not expect her to understand, therefore he was surprised when she said after a few moments of silence, "that is the journey one seeks for himself; I wish you good luck".

"I will only try part of the Elbe, I need to test my patience", he concluded.

"You probably find me still standing here when you are back to tell me how it was, unless you find yourself in the North Sea", she said, smiling.

-3-

She helped him release his boat off the quay, and that was the last sight of hers as he recalled, or at least that was what he thought.

He started up his boat's small engine and took off, navigating the short passage connecting to the Elbe. Within ten minutes the boat was born in the glorious river. He shut off the engine and let the sail lead the boat through its course. His guidance was the brain-based positioning system more than the on-board campus, for he had been through this course tens of times since he started sailing from this location. He ignored the fact that there are no two identical journeys with the same boat in the same river.

He noticed few boats ahead of his, sailing under the mercy of a weak wind, or the expectation of a good one, whatever the truth is. But his attention was in a different world. He sought knowledge all of his life and considered it the true path to freedom. How ignorance became a force driving human beings and to what end? He always had difficulty facing evil with evil believing Good must be powerful enough to lead our lives.

But how this can happen if the Truth continues to be elusive and people, most of them, are more inclined to deceit and pretense. Has the Time something to do with it? This cannot be, as the Truth is not temporary but timeless and permanent. Probably our nature is made out of lies, unless we look into eternity, if we can.

His thoughts kept fighting in his mind while his eyes were fixed into the grey of the horizon extended to infinity. Was he heading to the North Sea without recognizing it? It seemed that the wind was friendlier than indicated.

"Aren't there places in this world where a true will of peace could manifest itself? Can't I find one of such places within myself?", he desperately asked himself.

With more clouds accumulating above his head, he recalled Doris's warning to get into the North Sea in this uncertain weather. He needed to maneuver a large circle to reverse his course back to Wedel in case the weather is his real risk. His mind was occupied by different type of risk and he was not sure he has the knowledge to manage it, maybe it only requires the simple truth of life, if there is such a truth.

Absentmindedly, he found his hands on the sheet trimming the sail, tightening and easing until after sometime he could reverse the course; of the boat, not his course, at least not at that very moment. What kind of sail he needs to adjust for his life to take the truthful course?

He noticed that the few sailing boats around had already reversed their course ahead of him. Only big motor vessels were progressing up stream depending on their powerful engines where human invention confronts nature's ambiguity, assuming unannounced victory. They were seeking different course of truth. The glorious river was obviously accommodating them all.

While approaching the "Yachthafen" a small boat was visibly taking off to the river. He wondered who is onboard commanding such a small boat through uncertainty of weather while the day is coming to an end; as darkness started to befall. Is there yet another version of truth?

With the two boats approaching each other he immediately recognized the person standing on the smaller boat's deck, she was Doris. He fixed his sight at the Elbe enquiring: "is that part of your mystery?"

"Hay Doris, what are you up too, you did not seem intending to sail today, not that late in the day anyway?"

Her face reflected deep concern while saying: "there was an unusual aura around you today that made me a bit worried, I could not stand waiting any longer while the day is disappearing and your boat nowhere to be appearing, so I decided to find out for myself what it is all about"

"Do you expect the river is generous enough to reveal its truth to a small boat as such?" he said trying a smile, "let us get our boats to the marina before it is dark"

"Karl, your words to me earlier were intently telling Atlantic Ocean mystery not even North Sea, or part of the Elbe as you imagined. To be honest I did not expect your return so soon, and my curiosity took me by surprise deciding to follow your thoughts wherever they took me. Obviously, they did not take me too far and I found you on your return" she said, while redirecting her boat following him to the yacht harbor.

"You found my boat Doris, not me nor my thoughts, unless we are in a different reality and such things are aspects of only one possible truth", he sounded hopeful and optimistic, not sure she heard him.

She was touched by his tone, although his last words were absorbed by the awaken wind. That was what made her try to keep close; her boat, her thoughts and herself.

4. The blonde and the mudflat

-1-

One day in October a sunset was all what it took to change his world. Was that exasperation or just a hope? The beach of the small town was almost deserted. Berck-sur-Mer`s summer timers had left the Northern France uniquely isolated spot to the North Sea, to their much open and demanding world, or that what they think.

He strolled, his eyes were fixed at the horizon, his mind was swimming with waves of memories from the past and the future, and his feelings were on alert in a timeless world. He was ready for a change.

It was not a long beach compared to his home town Alexandria one. But it was equally fascinating, although for different reasons. Alexandria is located to the Mediterranean, different place, different time, nature speaks different language with the same meaning, at least for him.

He looked for a few seconds at the other side of the road to locate a cafe shop, named "Corne l'amour", one of many that were almost closed. He found it and felt hopeful when he saw a figure of a woman moving in and out. Probably she is. He inwardly smiled recalling her last time's greetings in French-accent English: "I hope to see you again"

-2-

Crossing a deserted road is a challenge unless you know already where, for him that was not unknown. He approached the cafe, already decided where to sit; to a table facing the timeless world.

She came after a few minutes with a warm smile, recognition carried her warmness. He sensed her existence although he was facing the beach and shifted to look at her.

Today she wore in green; with the blue from the eyes, the blonde of the hair, the white to the skin, the red on the nails; she represented her kind of victory to the world.

With her soft voice, she said: "I was not sure it was you when I located a single figure of a man approaching the cafe as a destination, getting closer provides assurance, would you like your regular cup of coffee?".

His eyes were fixed on her gentle face, but his mind was absorbing her question, trying to find an answer. "Yes please, you are kind enough to explain to me why the road is so deserted when it is a two-way," he said.

She was not taken by the mysterious question he put to her. It seemed that she had several chats with him that made her familiar with that sort of a man. "It is a matter of time, not direction. During summer there are many people, therefore, the road was one way. Now, it is direction free".

She was about to leave to get him his coffee, then she heard him saying: " I agree; therefore, the sea took back tens of meters, away from the road, I hardly can hear its whispers, sort of freedom too".

It took her few seconds to decide on her response, preferring a safe one. "You are observing the low tide effect, it is quite remarkable in Berck, the mudflat turns the beach into a unique scene. It happens regularly. No freedom to claim, it is nature," she said.

He smiled without looking at her and tried to challenge her, saying: "I can prove it to you in case you accompany me there".

She did not hesitate, this stranger was coming to show her what is visible at her sight, in a completely different way. She looked at her watch and said: "I will finish my work today within half an hour. I will bring you the coffee and wait on a couple of elders sitting inside, then after, accompany you to a world you do not understand, and probably won't".

He kept his eyes fixed at the horizon while the sun was descending. Probably she was right, he thought. Then, the softness of her voice came again while she was leaving, and she said: "By the way, my name is Segolene".

"Yes, I agree," he whispered to himself.

-3-

The sun completely disappeared as she presented herself to him, or probably because of that. The remaining traces of his redness, mixed with few high clouds scattered in the sky gave them sufficient guidance.

They were already walking bare-footed on the sand towards the sea that seemed going backwards as they progressed forward. He obviously did not mind that; imagining the sea was voluntarily allowing them enough room for their strolling, not alongside but bravely into it.

He was about to explain how man's gravity is more powerful than the moon's, but she was ahead of him saying: "I used to come here for the kite festival over the Easter weekend when I was young. I was absolutely charmed just by watching what was happening at low tide along the coast. People were strolling on the sand with their dogs, seals sunning themselves and birds going about their business, as if a new world for them was born".

It took a couple of minutes for him to say: "It is a change freely exercised; it is up to us to find a new world".

"It is all up to the mother Nature, the forces that control our world are beyond our comprehension, I study physics and I know what I am talking about," she said.

"Segolene, our world is supernatural, otherwise how we could be together in such a place in such a time?" he said deeply smiling.

It was breezing, but not chilly. The more they strolled closer to the waves' play the darker it became. "I do understand what you say, not with my mind, I need to be a bit irrational to reach you," she said.

He laughed accepting her conditions, and tried to detect a new connection, as he said:" I also like physics, gravity is the weakest of the four forces that control Matter. Although most indiscernible, it has tremendous effect on the whole universe".

She said with apparent satisfaction:" Now, you start to see the real world; we are not so free".

He said: "Oh my dear, you are fast claiming victory, we have not touched the waves yet". He added with a big smile she could not see: "You are Segolene, you are certain of attaining victory".

The seagulls were grouping, gaily repeating their special songs. He was fascinated by the whole existence surrounding and enveloping their beings.

She was quite until he noted:" I would love to be a seagull for one day. I am curious where they spend their nights".

That brought a laugh through her beautiful lips while saying: "You are really an amazing creature, are you certain of what you want?"

He said in not-very-visible seriousness: "I want to reach the depth of the water ahead of us".

She said: "My feet started to feel the wetness already, few meters or few moments and we will be partially in water".

"Probably the sea will retreat," he said.

"That is the farthest we can go, deeper, Moon gravity will insert its effect, even if it is the weakest force," she responded.

"Sure, it is, that is where our freedom should be tested," he continued.

"That is where my dress will get spoiled and I will be going home in a mess, is that your intention?" she flirted with him.

After a few minutes, the coldness of the water warned him, together with the slow change that was taken place as the Moon pronounced her existence.

" Think of the time not the place, Earth, Moon, Sun, all are there, it is when not where" he insisted.

She interrupted his flow of thoughts saying": You seem like our master of the sky, Eugene Boudin, who became famous as a marine painter and landscaper. On a mudflat, you are a live landscaper or shall I say **timescaper**?". She smiled to herself for manipulating an English word

Coming into deeper water; she slowed her paces until she almost stopped. "Now is the moment I concede to your view; dangerously clear, but we must go back all the same, shall we? That is unless you seek a separation not a change," she said.

Without hesitation, he gave her his hand and took back to the shore, with a clear but safe view.

-4-

It was the same time of same day of October, same cafe; same two elders were sitting inside.

The elder man looked affectionately at the woman's gentle face unaffected by the long years, its blue eyes brightened with intelligence, the blond hair was still shining with glory, the red color was manifested now on her lips, her skin whiteness was affected by light traces of time, she was still dressed in green.

He said quietly: "It is time they close here **dear; it** was the same time you promised to introduce me to your world many years ago, do you remember?"

She said with confidence although still with a question mark: "Yes, that was the moment of change you sought. I still hear you whispering to yourself, [yes, I agree] when I told you my name. What did you really mean then?"

5.   The Discoverers

She waited that long till he answered her question. The answer seemed not the one she waited for, so she stood up and went out for some private action. They were sitting by the beach looking to the far horizon while the sun was setting with glory and pride. He watched, alone, the far huge fireball descending into a world of oblivion and impossibility.

The question she asked was still hanging on his mind, and even the answer he offered. He also was not satisfied with his own answer. She had asked him „are you happy with your life?"

She was expecting in that romantic moment a declaration of his love and she is being the reason of all happiness in his life.

After a long silence and deep thinking his answer was "happiness is to freely accept your life". Why did not he just say: "yes, I am happy with you being around as my friend and lover?" But that he did not do and she felt sorry for asking the question. The question was still hanging there answerless, he also felt.

She came back wearing her swimming suit showing her great lovely body. It was her favorite hour for swimming. He looked at her admiringly and said: „yes dear, I am very happy with you being in my life"

She smiled at him so mischievously and said nothing, how he could freely accept his life with someone bound to him?

She jumped into the water waving to him invitingly. He was still attached to the fireball disappearing ceremoniously. She was also disappearing into the water trying to reach the unknown depth.

He was reading "The Discoverers" for Boorstin; the second part about earth and sea, and felt that he needs to discover that part of the sea containing her. Does he need a navigational chart to reach what he knows?

He put the book aside as it became dim and difficult to follow the lines clearly, and looked at her. She was floating on her back facing the sky where her vision lost its limitedness. She felt freely accepting her life. Also, the water was not so deep.

He approached the water slowly towards her, no longer was the fireball was there, instead a prevailing tail of redness. The water reached his shoulders and he was still heading to her direction. She could not see him in her position as the sea waves were embracing her. He became more involved while the water depth increased. The discoverers do not walk with feet nor fly with wings, they are happy creatures.

She felt his approach. Her eyes lost their concentration in the remoteness and she found herself turning around into the water facing him. He looked at her beautiful face wetted with the seawater, the bright eyes confessing her deep soul and his hands reached hers as the feet were losing contact with the sea bottom. They floated together farer from the beach while the darkness was befalling.

She warned him, are you sure of your direction?

He said, "it is becoming dark, not only to the sea. The direction is always your will, not your surroundings. Is your vision vanishing or only the eyes are discomforted?"

Upon his will, he started to get her into deeper water intending to reach the horizon. She wanted to laugh but instead she slightly smiled and started guiding him ashore.

He did not resist her moving away but found himself saying, "now, you definitely can find the answer to your question."

Then adding to himself, "the freedom to live is yet to be discovered."

6.   A Light of Life

He was at thirty-five thousand feet altitude looking from the airplane's window at the carpet of clouds stretched without limit. The clouds were moving and mixing creating all kinds of shapes and profiles. Were they foretelling a future of a day he was obsessed with? He knew of foretelling cards and stones, even tea leaves, coffee, palms, and stars of course, but he never heard of foretelling clouds. Between being asleep and awake his consciousness was floating. The link to his dream was the one he never lost. His brain found it difficult to decide which world it belonged to, while the clouds keep foretelling him a story hard to believe.

"What am I doing here?" he asked himself. "Where am I going?" he questioned his reality. The stewardess approached him asking whether he liked something to drink. That meant he was not in a dream, not exactly. Was it possible that he believed his imaginative world and just followed its course in a real world? What if he found himself where he wanted to be but not with whom he imagined to meet? Something twisted his heart and accelerated its beats, when the brain tried its logic. It is the moment when a dream is aborted by a sudden cross of a reality. "Do I want to live out of my dream and without it?" again he questioned his will.

In the morning hours he found himself heading to the airport and boarding the plane he booked two weeks ago. Then, the will was there driven by certainty he did not know how to explain. Is it possible to explain a certainty of a dream? The pilot announced the starting descent of his plane to prepare for landing, which made him regain his self-confidence or so he imagined.

The passenger who was sitting next to him smiled and asked whether he will stay in the city or take to a connecting flight. Maybe his neighbor wanted to confirm his attachment to the same world of others. Was he really belonging to that same world? Whether he was staying or taking a connecting flight, he definitely was not belonging, at least not at that moment of time, at least not for today. He found himself smiling back politely to his neighbor and responding that he will seek a way to reach his destination. Travelling is a marvelous way to discover our intentions and possible destinations. He tried to convince himself. A light reflected from his window on "In one person"; a novel by John Irving, he was trying to read during the four hours flight, an attempt to connect to a world not made of dreams, not of hard facts, a world of his creation, or so he imagined.

-2-

The early hours of the morning were telling her it was a new day being born. The same was apparent to every being, everywhere, in so many different languages. She decided the day will be new only if it was born specifically for her. She did not accept to be addressed as one of many. She felt the world owes her more than just the early hours of a day. And, that was exactly what the world intended to do today, to address her, and only her. That was how she got up full of certainty and trust, at least for those few moments until she became fully awake.

The dream has fed her with clarity of what to come. The dream was based on deep self-realization, she had never experienced before. She spent the late hours of her last night reading his hundreds of messages and what she responded to each one, asking how was it possible that she rediscovered herself through his written words. No one single word was verbally exchanged between them for the days of her journey with him through herself.

She took her shower, dressed up while her first coffee of the day was being consumed. As her working hours were running, disappearing in the past, exposing the coming ones to a future still to be born; her whole being was bound in a timeless world, imagining one moment only. It was the moment she will meet him on the platform of the train station. The platform she did not know which, as the train would come from the unknown.

How he would look like? Will she be able to recognize him? What if she missed him? What if he did not show at all, breaking his promise? The most agonizing question was what if he really comes and she was able to recognize him then the thousands of words exchanged between them became meaningless, when the timeless world changes to present and the day becomes not hers? Wouldn't it be safer to keep in dream and avoid challenging it be the unknown?

Energy Management was the topic of her lecture to the class today. She was not feeling comfortable talking about such a topic with insufficient practice, although, in every occasion she was admired. Is her ability to communicate exceeds her knowledge of what to communicate? Is our self-awareness so vital to connect our souls? Is that being why she follows her intuition and not her rational? Her mind was mixing her lecture of the day with her life promise.

Did she realize that there is only one self for each being and only with more dimensions we can travel the unknown and find the timeless world? Her dream was rich of such dimensions, she noticed, and she sought more, to travel deeper and to create her own day.

-3-

Many times, he crossed these airport halls and corridors towards the connected train station. Every time he used to observe something new. This time it seemed the whole airport is new to him, was it because his eyes were wandering in a different world?

Only his feet knew how to reach the train station while his mind was completely captured in a world of emotions. "What would be your emotions when you were promised to meet yourself?" he questioned his reality. That is why his whole being became bound by one single moment of time. That is why his mind failed to free itself.

The big overhead screen in front of him showed his train schedule, to which platform it will arrive, and when to depart. It was platform 6 where he should wait for a vehicle to take him with hundreds of others to the same destination. But his destination was characterized by more than a place and probably different than the other hundreds. It was destined by the moment he will meet her, not only by the station or the platform she might be waiting on.

It was November and the weather was cold, he walked over the platform with eyes fixed on the hanging watch. Does the time go slower with lower temperature? He found a place where smoking is allowed and started to engage his patience with a different aspect than time.

But of course, the watch, the train, the temperature and the smoking are representing aspects of their own where destination of a man is completely irrelevant. That made him curious, especially when the train arrived in time and he could find his seat as booked.

He got back to his reading habit while the train was gaining its maximum speed. It is important to reach self-awareness, but is he prepared to accept what he is? Will she accept limitation of his world as a boundary of her freedom? Wouldn't it be safer to keep the world of words and the world of acts apart? Dreams are not made of either of those two worlds. And to prove the reality we gamble more than our happiness, when we add the unknown and expect self-awareness.

-4-

It was 5pm and her seminar came to an end. His train was scheduled to arrive at 7.00pm. It is a walking distance to the train station. She felt that many reasons would hold her from being there in time, and that two hours to reach the arrival platform are not enough.

She hurried to her room in the hotel which took just few minutes, but the delay of the elevator made her heart quickens its beats. She rushed into her room and threw the heavy training stuff of the day on the nearest table. She looked at the wall mirror in the front of the door to check her clothes. She decided on the color of her dress to wear today many days ago, but again she was in question, did she make the right choice? Will the green she decided reflect his expectation in its degree and extent? He will certainly notice it and find a meaning; he always tries to find a meaning of anything and everything. He thinks he can control the world of words while the world of words seems controlling him.

It was a ten minutes walking distance from her hotel to the train station which she took in five minutes, although she knew that she will reach a bit early for his train to arrive. Probably she preferred waiting on the destiny and the unknown rather than the mathematics of time and distance.

Strange power was attracting her to where a question is coming more than an answer that is sought. "Is it really my foot that carries me to a place I only recall from a dream?" she asked herself. "I am swimming with a kind wave to a safe shore that I do not see yet, but I am certain it is there" she resonated with her consciousness.

The train station was crowded as usual at that hour of the day. People were on their way back to their homes after one working day had come to an end. Others were stopping in as it was here their last wave ended up, hoping for another wave to bring them somewhere different. Are we living through time waves?

She admitted to herself a feeling of happiness because it was not an ended working day that made her way to the station, neither a time wave that is desperate for a reborn. It is a characteristic of fate that is not bound by time or place.

Her happiness was pure and unconditional of him being here or there; his existence has connected her dream and reality that does not need a proof. That is why she felt peaceful and joyful because of the discovery of her truth became possible. A trace of sadness she felt because of the long way that she had taken.

The minutes remained for his train to arrive felt as pleasurable as painful. All birth moments are as such.

-5-

He stepped down from the last wagon of his train. The whole platform was stretched out in front of him with people coming out from all wagons in the same time mixed with those who were waiting there either to step in or to meet someone.

He recalled the stretched carpet of clouds he followed from the plane trying to read their prophecy. His heart was beating faster in his chest while his eyes were trying to search for her face and his feet were slowly progressing. Could it be that she was waiting on the wrong platform, or misread the arrival time, or was held in a traffic, or disbelieved her dream?

Like first light of the morning when darkness starts to vanish, her face had come to his sight. Like life when out of the unknown triggers the first beat in a heart, he became aware of his arms around her. The time passed while he kept holding her, will always be a mystery. He only noticed that the platform became again quieter, and her shaking transformed to relaxation. Was she crying from the effect of surprise or the happiness of being certain?

"No words are needed when one meets herself" she whispered.

"All words are required to interpret such a meaning" he imagined himself saying.

"I know your fascination of the world of words" she kept saying.

"It was the world allowed us to meet with each other and each with himself" he continued his self-dialogue.

" We still need to know each other in other worlds?" she was one step ahead of him.

"We met ourselves, we can be in all worlds with no fear of doubt or uncertainty" he confidently admitted while his hand held hers.

They walked back to her hotel thinking of all the worlds they will discover together. Their happiness was not a dream although born through one. Their light of life started with self-awareness. No other guarantee for a safe end is possible.

7.   River of Glory

It was warm as usual during this time of the year, or may be a little bit warmer. The absence of the Earth`s universal source of heat did not affect that much. Sometimes absence emphasizes existence. So, almost everyone had got himself to the riverside, the permanent source of protection and comfort.

The darkness was total, except for some street lamps and the dreamy light reflected from some sailing boats. That mixing between complete darkness and dim lighting gave the sitters and walkers a sort of unreal existence, vague and undecided. A dream about to be rational or reality dressed in the probable and things yet to be. Every moment, more of such figures joined the distributed masses. The effect of absence was conversely increasing. Now, additionally two figures entered the stream.

The river had never rejected new comers. It was always the reason of unity and eternity for man and land. The two figures were heading north, intentionally or not, nobody knows. When they passed through a street lamp they could be recognized as man and woman. So, the unity achieved by the river manifested itself again as the momentous lighting told, as the continuous darkness, that enveloped them, did.

She whispered to him after a long silence," I can clearly understand why this country was the gift of that river ". Her eyes were fixed on the water`s surface in persistence to fathom the depth of her statement. It seemed that they were catching up with an old dialogue.

He shook his head and looked into her face trying to trace the looks and said," I believe that the man was the hero of that drama, he created his own river and offered the gift to his kind ".

She followed her own thoughts saying," your grandfathers built up their civilization mainly due to their close observance of the river. They could measure the time more accurately than others through thousands of years because the nature offered them that magnificent location, this is only one thing to refer to ".

He smiled kindly as she was imagining him saying," are you saying that the Americans are reaching the planets because their part of sky is more adventurous? "

She didn't answer for a while, then she said," to do great things, man needs agreeable nature and a welcoming world ".

They were passing by some people who were nursing at their tea cups. The looks were exchanged transferring the first interaction between personalities. The looks were followed by the welcoming smiles and invitation for a cup of tea. She touched his hand for approval. The warmness of the night developed her thirst, the continuous dialogue sought a change of taste. She was also a tea addict.

The folk offered them a place to sit and a cup of tea for each. An old man asked him in their native language," she looks like a foreigner, from which country she is? ".

He tried to satisfy his curiosity by saying," she is a friend ". Then added," the river is so much crowded with people tonight, it is obviously due to the warm weather ".

The man just smiled and said," The weather has always guided the people to the river, warm or cold, he is like a father to us or may be a mother, all the same ".

A middle-aged woman added," My best times I spent walking by the river building my own dreams, or burying them ".

When he translated what they said to his friend, she said," I am not in contradiction with you, if we are talking about the same thing ".

They thanked the folk for the tea and resumed their way back to where they parked the car.

Before they reached their final destination, she struggled to tell him," nothing can take you out of that river, nothing can take it out of you, are you now satisfied? ".

He looked at her face lighted by the city over lighting, showing every piece of emotion inflaming in her, and wished if he would be just there in her innermost self,

streaming through her source of beauty.
This would save him the answer!

8.   Riding to Self-Consciousness

The train started its journey from Alexandria at noon, as usual, heading to Cairo, about 220 km south. It should stop only once at about the middle, in a city called Tanta. Most of the passengers were destined to the end.

The last one has jumped in the train just seconds before it left. He was lucky enough to find a free seat in one of the first-class wagons. Once he located the empty place, he rushed towards and occupied it with such tremendous feeling of relief. He then searched his suitcase for the book he had kept there, opened it and started reading as if it was the actual reason of trying so hard to reach that specific place of the movable world of a train.

Before long, the train gained its steady speed. Also, the last passenger became so involved in his world, he could only be distracted by the waiter asking if he would wish some refreshments. When he got disturbed by the waiter, he started to grasp his surroundings and the meaning of the place. He noticed for the first time that he had a neighbor by the window and she was a woman. Most of the passengers were occupied by a talk or taken by an immediate nap.

He stared at the waiter and said absent-mindedly, "would you ask the lady first, please?"

The waiter smiled politely and noted, "The lady has already ordered some tea."

The passenger said in a matter of haste, "then some tea also for me, thank you."

Before his intention to resume reading took place, he heard his neighbor asking, "Do you know how many stops the train has to do before reaching Cairo?"

He turned his head to look at her before putting an answer. Her face transmitted to him an encouragement to talk mixed with curiosity of what he will say.

"Only one stop, at Tanta.", he answered her.

She did not seem to be of the napping type, so she tried to release him for more talking.

"Normally, I do not ride train in my travels, I prefer driving." she added.

After a long thought he said, "It depends upon your purpose of travel."

Cautiously, she said, "I think everybody travels, to be in somewhere which he isn't. The faster he will to be there the better."

She seemed to be in her early thirties, something to talk about how fast she wants to be there.

When he didn't respond for a while, she asked rather reluctantly, "Am I interrupting your reading?"

"With your last statement you are not." he said.

As she could not understand his last statement, she kept her silence, then he offered an explanation, "I also travel to be in somewhere else, but no specific place. I use my books as the fastest way to be there."

She started to feel his strangeness, but that did not deter her. She decided that her journey would be more amusing than she dreamed of.

"Then it makes no difference to you whether the train is heading to Cairo or Luxor. Does it?" she inquired.

She felt no hesitation in him saying, "It depends upon the kind of knowledge I am after, which is the book I am involved with."

The waiter came back with the requested tea. She tried to use the interruption to steer the dialogue back to normal. "Tea is very popular, don't you think?" she said

"Yes! Driving maintains privacy but does not offer independence." he said, still minding her own words.

She sensed his entanglement with her way of expressing things and found herself saying, "I do not doubt my independence, as much as tolerated by the society"

After an assured look at her left hand he said, "Even as a married woman?"

Confidently she answered, "Especially as one. But I must admit that mine is not a general case. My husband is a researcher in the University of Cairo, he is totally dedicated to his work. I fully support him and do not permit myself to burden him with my problems. We sometimes live in Alexandria; he lives most of his time in Cairo."

He said after some thought, "He certainly is a lucky man. But you have mixed independence with freedom."

The train was eating its way through the Nile delta with that vast landscape of greenness on both sides. Water canals and ditches stretched like veins and arteries. Animals of different kinds were helping giving life new chances and possibilities. The man still the focus of existence.

When she didn't comment on his last words, he correctly assumed her confusion, so he added, "I also have my own obligations, and it makes no difference marital or otherwise. I doubt my independence, but not my freedom."

She thought for few seconds and said, "in a train with an anonymous, who cares for obligations. I think it could be a true opportunity to honestly face oneself. But the two and half hour might not be enough."

He vaguely said, "My trip might not be ended by that time. My destination is not yet known to me. Probably I picked the wrong book."

She immediately said, "Or the wrong train."

He admired her sophistication and tried to express it by saying, "but definitely I got the right neighbor."

"Because I am keeping you from your reading?" she argued.

"The book is not necessarily what I keep by hands." he explained.

She looked at the tea cup in her hands and then at the moving objects outside the train`s world, her thoughts were lost somewhere else. This man sitting so near to her is so far and different from the one who is far there and intimately related and connected. What is really moving and what is constant? She couldn't tell. When she saw him rushing to the free seat beside her, she couldn't decipher his face, though she felt a peculiar feeling of attraction. She promised herself to resolve his mystery, as the travelling time lasts. Now, she became more lost in his mystery than gaining him to her clarity. One thing was secretly growing inside her, the attraction she felt at the very beginning.

The train conductor reached their seats to check their tickets. She showed hers and he offered him some money. The conductor inquired about his destination: Tanta or Cairo. He said he would prefer Cairo with two-way ticket. The conductor gave him what he asked for with little show of astonishment, and left. It seemed he has some good experience of the human peculiarities.

He noticed his neighbor's engagement to her own world and preferred not to interfere. He was used to people experiencing such strangeness after a little talk with him and as usual become disenthralled to continue. Then he can regain his impaled privacy. Was it sort of self-defense or defiance?

He was about to resume reading and get back to this timeless world when he heard her saying, "the train is crossing Rashid branch of Nile. I feel I am also crossing some sort of a bridge, at least my mind. It has been taken by your way of thinking to a different area of reality. With so few words you opened hard questions carefully avoided by almost everyone."

His eyes followed the bridge which the train was crossing. The water was split by the train as if touched by a magic cane. He thought about her courage to resume the discussion, something he didn't expect.

"Everybody feels some loneliness. At some certain point of time or place, he or she, discovers and has to face it. Some do escape, others have the courage to admit and deal with it. Is that the bridge you feel crossing by now?", he inquired.

She felt such an unexpected feeling of sheer happiness, that someone a stranger to her can read her and naturally explain what was shyly concealed from others no matter how intimate they are.

The train had already approached Tanta and took a halt. It is one of the biggest crossroads stations in the country and very busy with people and interests.

"I wonder with so many railways crossing each other a train can find its right way", she said.

"It is the advantage of being directed," he observed.

She thought for some time and said," I prefer to make my own mistakes. That is the meaning of freedom you meant a while ago, isn't it? "

The train had already moved leaving Tanta behind, the distance to Cairo was becoming less, the time remained was shorter, unless she interferes with its direction!

When he offered no answer she added, "But I can't explain my increasing feeling of dependence on our discussion, or rather on your way of putting things in place. The remaining hour is hardly sufficient to satisfy my curiosity."

As if to confirm her point he said, "The quality of time is more important than its duration, besides, it is our decision to end our journey at a certain point. It is another way to do mistakes." He smiled.

"May be, I should get a ticket back with you. I am not used to a loose end," she thought to herself.

He seemed closer to her by saying, "you feel stronger and more dominating your destiny through the journey because your obligations, if you remember, were left behind. Once the train slows down at its last stop the moment of triumph vanishes and the old self is back. Then the husband or wife or else ironically emerges in another sort of reality. That is why I avoid determining destination points. I might as well step down in Cairo keeping my part in the bargain."

She was bewildered, it was not reasonable what this stranger was trying to tell her. How could her choices be so deceiving? And only within a short trip by a random train the self-determination and strong will can be experienced. And then the choice is to ignore the wonderfully revealed truth and disappear into self-oblivion because the train is destined to Cairo.

The train was actually approaching Cairo. She didn't know what to decide especially after he declared the possibility to quit the train in Cairo. There was still a lot going inside her world which needs guidance to clarity by this man. How can she guarantee her needlessness of him after he was mixed with the unknown masses?

The questions were rushing inside her head taking over the will to control, while the train controls were at stop on its platform at Cairo railway station.

He looked at her in kindness and said, "we still have some time till the train goes back to Alexandria. I hope you accept my invitation for another cup of tea in the station café. It is a transition place between the two worlds. There we will decide, if we haven't already done, our next stop."

9. Courage to love

The road was long but smooth. The car was not comfortable but reliable. The weather was unexpectedly beautiful, clear, sunny and dry. The two occupants of the car were so full of life and hopes, what a journey!

Last night, when he received her at the airport, she expressed her dream to be in a real desert. Today his ability to realize her dreams was put to test. He decided to take her somewhere in the western desert. There she will be enveloped in the unlimited. That is how man measures his outmost.

In the beginning of this journey, she looked in his eyes for a longer time than she used to, a sign of communicating her full trust. It is what a man, realizing a life dream, needs. To respond to such a moment of subtlety, he touched her face so affectionately and smiled.

After the town was left behind, he said, "now we will take the coast road for some hundred kilometers then shift towards south where your dreamy place spreads beyond recognition"

She knew his old love to the sea, so she smiled and said:" last time we spent a lovely day on Sokhna beach. Do you still remember

our swimming while the darkness was befalling?"

"It was not the darkness that got me nearer
to the unknown, it was your love", said he.

She said not at all be taken by his obscurity:"
if you had got us any deeper, we would have
lost our way back, so I had to tempt you ashore"

He said:" women are always the better partners, they have been bequeathed life creativity,
so safety is their essential instinct. Men are after
the reason; they are the cause of agony for themselves and the world. But that does not include
you and me"

She laughed from her deep heart, and said:"
because I am after the reason and you are a cre-
ator, is it not every artist a sort of one?"

"Before getting ourselves involved any deeper, let us get the car enough fuel for the whole
trip" he said while shifting the car towards the
coming fuel station.

She stepped out and went to the lady's room.
When she came back, he was ready to resume
driving. She offered him some refreshments she
bought from the mini market there. He felt a

rare happiness at that moment, because she did not ask him what he would prefer, nevertheless he got it.

He resumed driving westward. The Mediterranean coast was to their right with its especially blue water extended as far as their eyes could take, except where some of the tourism villages were constructed imposing their limitedness on the real as well as the imaginative. She noticed his annoyance when his vision was hindered, then she said:" don't get annoyed, the sea is not hidden nor has disappeared, such constructions inconveniently hindering your vision will never touch its vastness within you."

He was looking at the other side of the road when he said:" maybe the desert has the right answer."

He kept silent for a long time. She shared his silence. It seems they chose a different world to communicate their thoughts and feelings. The car folded its way approaching "El Alamein". While she reflects on the desert's outskirts stretched alongside the road, she broke her silence suddenly asking him:" why don't we cross the desert through an unmarked road and discover what is hidden from the world? The car is reliable and full of fuel."

As she broke already their special world of silence, he replied:" we`ll soon approach a dirt road used by the oil companies operating in the heart of the western desert, we can drive parallel to that road."

She appeared at a loss, therefore he explained:" this dirt road is randomly marked up by stones on both sides avoiding sand dunes and gullies, to guide truck drivers to where these companies are camped. It extends tens or hundreds of kilometers."

"I did not mean to take a parallel road, I meant to discover our own road," she said after his explanation.

He knew how much dangerous her wish was, especially if they found themselves in the heart of desert without campus or a marked road while the night's darkness befalling them. In the meantime, he realized the challenge in her tone, expressing her strong wish to face the unknown. Should his love to her exceeds his fear for her? Should he ignore his responsibility for her safety to fulfill what she was wishing for?

He kept silent while driving off the main road towards the desert following a trodden dirt road. Then, he suddenly departed the dirt road and speeded up westward until they disappeared in the desert with all the markers of the dirt road lost to their vision and consciousness. Her face beamed with joy while she was seeking his right hand to kiss it, allowing him only his left on the steering wheel.

"My heart controls my mind at this moment, believe me when we decide to go back, we must find a way", he admitted.

"Let us watch the sunset surrounded by this limitless desert, never be afraid to be part of nature, our return is influenced by when not where", she said with excitement.

"There is a reason for our existence my lady, we have not been aimlessly created, therefore we must not waste our lives in search for a road in the desert", he sympathized her enthusiasm and tried to philosophy.

"Are you afraid that we die, lost in the magic of such magnificent endless desert?", she daringly asked after short contemplation.

He could not find an answer to her question except going ahead towards the far unattainable horizon. The sun commenced its descent, creating from surrounding sand dunes their shadows, a new alphabet for the existence to communicate with.

He stopped the car to watch the sunset. A scene that caused resonance to their heart beats. In that moment, she took him in her arms and kissed his lips. The moment extended until it vanished with the sun, in its mysterious fascinating world.

Within one hour the twilight became dusk. Darkness was spreading, enveloping their whole surroundings, causing the stars to illuminate and fascinate. Gradually, a depthless boundless world embraced them, a world full of secrets mans' mind is unable to fathom. In the darkness the desert was swallowed, the place was absorbed in a time not observable by their watches.

They were both silent, speechless and captivated by the glory of the moment until his fingers touched her. He whispered in her ear, avoiding to disturb the desert's silence:" I love you." That was his answer to a question he never dared to answer.

10. Dreams' Prisoners

He saw her, so clearly and purely. The eyes illuminated with love, the forehead shining with delight, the silver smooth skin pulsing with compassion.

"If clarity is attainable in dreams why do we need reality?" he asked himself.

She wanted to assure him her existence, irrelevant to their world, so she approached him till he could feel her warmness. The beautiful neck inclined, the lovely hair touched her back, and the look was full of longing and desire. He did not resist the invitation furiously expressed in her lips. The kiss lasted beyond the calculated time; the life is more powerful because it is the only expression of existence.

They went on a road not known to them in reality, saw places for the first time and met people from another world. As if this world of dreams is capable to fulfil; where the visible one fails.

Their hands were tightened together when she said, "I am sure we are in a dream and not in the real world ".

He was drugged by her scent and hand smoothness when he said, 'my dilemma is to relive a dream you never know about ".

Her sadness showed when she said, "why human beings cannot meet in a dream as they do in reality? Then everyone would get his share of happiness, tirelessly ".

'Why do you remind us of pains? They should be forgotten in that rare moment ", he said.

"Yes, like forgetting a rare moment with just a wake up! "she remarked.

'You will never know of our meeting and the entwined hands ", he added.

" And this taste of a kiss, only you might recall, I am so sorry ", she said.

"You know, who enjoys the taste longs for the impossible ", he insisted.

" Are you certain of me not dreaming the same dream at that moment? ", she hopefully inquired.

'If that is possible then I will go to that place in reality guided by your spirit and shared clarity ", he delightedly said.

'Without arrangement? ", her reality persisted.

'If it was possible in dreams, why not ever? ", his dream fancied.

-2-

He woke up, remembering what he experienced in his dream; specially the taste of her lips. A feeling of disappointment and emptiness enveloped his soul. Unknown sadness was suppressing what was left of deep happiness and satisfaction. What had happened was only an echo of his imaginative subconscious driven by illusion of deep desires. Then he recalled his promise to her to go to the same place as in the dream. His mind ridiculed him listening to a promise of a dream. The hope to fulfill a promise pushed his sadness away.

-3-

He prepared himself to a meeting he does not know when or where. The time in the dream was spring, the place was paradise. Should he enhance his steps or slow down? Where to stop for wait? He implored his mind to think illogically for once, in a day that might realize his promise dream.

In someplace his consciousness had taken him to halt and enjoy the heavy mask of trees alongside the road. He stopped and expectedly listened to the next moments. He wished to share the surrounding creatures their philosophy and be part of their unknown world.

While he was drowning himself in the beauty of the scene, footsteps gradually approached him. He could feel their destination is his. Then the steps reached him, and the hand offered to him was hers.

She was saying, "My belief won my doubt, my love guided me after the mind quitted itself".

He tried to control his emotions saying, "The miracle is not our meeting, it is our belief in it".

Flirtatiously she asked, "Shall I tell you what guided me to you in my dream?"

He intellectually responded, "What shall we gain from repeating ourselves?"

She insistently continued, "But meeting in place and time must be different from meeting in dream world".

He said quite confidently, "We made it indifferent." *let me enjoy your* "Then added, *being with me in the same* moment and place, it will be my proof to the real world that it cannot est-range us".

She said no word but turned to him with complete satisfaction that his belief of a dream' promise made it possible for hers to come true. But he has never doubted her as promise dream.

11. Unity of Equals

"So, this is where you meet yourself?" she said; more as a statement than a question.

Her face was reflecting the affection of sun rays of a beautiful day of January, with eyes projecting the sea waves with millions of water-drops when crashing with the rocks obstructed their way to the beach. The eyes were containing the world of a sea. Her consciousness seemed totally absorbed by the soothing white noise, creation of the continuous try of sea waves to clear their way and free themselves, and probably those who watch them.

As she was not expecting an answer, her mind just flew with the eternity of a sky that spread where the sea seems at end. Around her, few people were spreading; some of them with their children, reminding her that that part of the picture was real, but did she notice?

She felt that her whole being was focused in the man beside her, whose attention was overwhelmed by the eternity she also was lost in. She wondered whether his world ever separated from the universe around them.

-2-

Everything around him was moving on its own. The waves were coming hitting the rocks persistently; having no other target but to reach where they announce their triumph. The sea was changing with every drop flying in the air. It composed a monotone music in a continuous melody, the ears never get bored to listen to. The clouds were lazily moving endorsing never ending shapes of the sky. The wind was carrying to those who feel it a fragrance that captures their senses with absolute sensuality. The sun was descending to his new cradle for a continuous rebirth. There was no randomness or peculiarity, all was moving in tandem in nonending symphony.

It was not unusual for him to absorb such a unity and feel its hidden harmony. His thoughts were also moving like the waves in front and the clouds above. His feelings were sensing the absolute scent, and touching its color. The unusual was the completeness of his being in such a moment that made him swim in a world of his own. A world of no need to a language. A world he does not feel lonely or be alone. A world where there is no sadness or sorrow or regret.

She was looking in his face trying to locate where his true being was.

He felt her eyes on him and looked at her passionately and said; "Yes, this is where I meet myself, because I meet you".

She pressed his hand with hers and did not have to say, "I love you", as no language was needed in their world.

12.   A Moment of Time

He was always fascinated by great men. That was since his consciousness was able to establish a link with the real life. That means since he became able to read!

Carlyle's book "On Heroes, Hero-Worship, and the Heroic in History" opened a wonderful world to his imagination. "What it takes to become a great man; a prophet, a revolutionist, a poet or a writer?" he kept wondering. And, he kept reading and searching.

He read "The Story of My Experiments with Truth" and found out why "Ghandi" was a great man. "The Long Way to Freedom" explained to him how "Mandela" was powerful while facing the Wrong. The Good signified through the two narratives; "The Life of Mohamed" and "The Life of Jesus" confirmed to him that a human being can really be great. Especially when he read the lives of "Stalin", "Mao" and "Hitler" and recognized the abyss of Evil man is also capable to plunge into. Then he discovered the sense of beauty as exhibited to him through arts and the creative power of artists.

What makes any of these men different, he kept thinking. Do they have different sequence of their genome than most of their race? Or, their environment excluded them for singularity? Or, there is a unique impulse triggered within their existence by the Unknown, which they can only obediently respond to?

How could the oil and canvas in Picasso's hands turn into paintings like "Guernica", "The Weeping Woman", "Portrait de Dora Maar" and many others? He did not believe in magic and no one was able to tell him the secret of being great. But he did not know that the answer to his mysterious question was probably closer to him than he imagined.

-2-

She was taken by the beauty of the face and the look of the eyes. The head was a brilliant model of fine structure. The nose was well placed above the generous mouth with its full lips. The chin accomplished a delicate balance with a centerline going to the gracious forehead foretelling a musical note of symphonic ratios. A look resembled the look of a racing horse full of trust and pride that transcends triumph or defeat. Or it resembled the fixed look of a lion who obeys nothing but his own nature, or the look of an elephant that reflects deep patience and mercy an outcome of unyielding power. Or all of them together and more. She longed to un-interruptedly look at this face and sink into these eyes and try her creative will.

-3-

He was sitting at a table next to the window. In front of him a cup of coffee untouched. A book on "The Hidden Life of Trees" was laid o-pen next to it. His sight seemed fixed at a point of space its time passed away.

When he sensed her existence, he thought she was the waitress coming to take his order for lunch. Instead, he found an unfamiliar face with a smile directed to him.

Before his cognitive system started to wan-der, he heard her saying: "I apologize for intru-ding your world. I only hope for a moment of your time."

Her warm smile and kind voice made him smile back. He said: "It is a lovely day when man is asked what he is able to give. May I offer you a cup of coffee? I have not ordered my lunch yet."

She considered this as an invitation to sit in the empty chair in front of him. "That depends on how persuasive I can be" she said while her eyes were trying to absorb his face like a portrait by Renoir.

It was a quite bistro which he regularly visited to take his lunch or rather to spend his lunch time, a walking distance from his workplace.

"Actually, I need your help", she said; not to keep him wondering.

What help he might possibly able to offer to this highly willed lady? He kept silent, just looking at her eyes as they were fixed kindly on his face.

"I am a sculptor", she started. "I have been searching for an inspiration to start a new work until I saw your face. It triggered a glow in my fingers. I cannot wait to hold my chisel and start carving."

"Inspiration is a mysterious motivation specially to create an artistic work, no one can explain", he said. Then added: "but I still cannot see how I can help you".

"1 would like to invite you to visit my gallery and see how I try to define the mystery of life using different kind of stones. I want to try the granite this time, as an expression and communicative way of life. Will you help me for one moment of time?"

-4-

The place was a completely different world than his. A large room with scattered tables and cupboards. Different sizes and types of stones were stacked here and there; soapstone, alabaster, serpentine, limestone and sandstone. Some of the partially finished carved sculptures were put away from the room center where a rather big untouched piece of granite stood or laid on a metal table. On the ground under the metal table few chisels, rakes, rasps and hammers were stored.

While trying to absorb the surrounding environment and grasp its meaning, he suddenly asked her: "what does it really take to make a great sculptor?".

The question of greatness was haunting him wherever he met a human being with creative power. He listened to different answers and was not convinced by any. Now he got a chance for one more answer.

She did not try to hide her surprise from his sudden question. After a few moments of considering how to reply, she said: "l thought you will allow me some time to make my sketches that can help creating my next sculpture".

"I don't see any complete sculpture around here to think of the next one", he said noticing her avoidance to answer his question.

She looked at him thoughtfully and said: "Probably that answers your question. He is great who completes his work".

They were now standing looking at each other, between them the granite piece. He came closer and touched it while composing his question: "Granite is a very hard kind of stone; how you can make it lean to your thoughts and feelings?".

She approached the other side of the table where he was standing, then said: "Technically I use carbide-tipped tools and diamond saws and grinder to carve it. More difficult and harder is to obtain the right meaning within it. That requires inspiration or revelation".

"So, you think whoever completes his or her sculpture is a great sculptor, and of course, a sculpture that reveals the true meaning of its stone or its sense of beauty to my understanding?" he said.

Then added as if he was listening to a voice within him: "Is that also the case for the painter with his painting and the poet with his poem and the writer with his book and the social reformist with his message? And how can we identify a complete work? With a world in a continuous change, all rules and codes are constantly changing, even religious rules and moral codes. That means a great man is relative to the time when he initiated his work and the land where he faced his challenges and confronted his fate. Also, to what extent his work improved life of his community within the scale of human race and its course of evolution".

She was looking at him fascinated by the expression of his face during his self-dialogue. He seemed deeply engaged in a non-interrupted debate that started far earlier than this moment. He seemed appraising her as the sum of her scattered sculptures, incomplete as he may have considered. She dared to look at her granite stone, imagining how it will look like one day.

"I think the questions that we have no hope to find an answer should not be asked. They are like work that will never get completed", she volunteered.

"Is your piece of granite so hard for your thoughts and feelings to produce a complete work?", he continued debating.

She smiled and said in a mysterious way: "You gave me more than a moment of your time. Hence, I have a hope to answer this question but not today".

-5-

How many days or years had passed since she got that moment of his time and more? How deep were her thoughts, how strong were her emotions as she progressed in revealing the secret of her granite and creating her masterpiece of a sculpture?

She stood in front of it, proud of her achievement; for nothing was missed of the expressions of his face while he was pouring his thoughts out and her existence was vibrating with his.

Was it a great sculptor? Was it a complete one? She was unable to tell. But she could tell where it had been exhibited and for how long and how many visitors were standing in front of it taken by its beauty.

It had travelled to "Albertina Museum" in Vienna, to "Petit Palais" in Paris, to "Galleria Borghese" in Rome and was still on demand. Some art critiques and famous magazine art viewers defined her as an expressionist, others argued her surrealism and some others imagined her symbolism.

When she was asked what she wanted to communicate to the world through her masterpiece, she answered that she can only hope to find an answer!

And, she kept asking herself how her life would look like if that moment of his time had extended to a lifetime.

13.   The day I met my Sorrow

It was Saturday night when I received the phone call. I rushed out immediately, for it might be the last call. Despite this had been frequently repeated during the last six months, I did not allow myself the rest of habit, for any time might be the one. Why did I expect a difference with the last call? What could be this difference, if ever? I dared not to think. Should there be a difference between a life that lasts and when it lasts not? I had no time to face any mind persistence, there was only time, if any, to resist self-limitations.

The streets were crowded as usual, not with expectations and possibilities but rather with people and cars. What do you expect of a road that leads to the wrong end and a time that is consumed to reach emptiness?

When I reached our home, I have learnt that he was unconsciously taken to the hospital. The streets to the hospital were narrower and quitter. People were looking at me transmitting not too much feeling. In some respect, I felt lonely.

Entering the hospital gave me additional feeling of uneasiness and unjustified drive for resistance. A nurse indicated the room where he is, a sign outside the corridor read IC. The air around was transmitting different types of waves, invisible world was touching and overlapping with the visible one.

He was lying on a bed dimensionally incredible. But dimensions in such places are measured by the need. Life supporting equipment and instruments were around and into him trying to show some influence on the unknown.

The doctor was looking extensively at him when I came into the room. The doctor noticed and shook his head knowingly. It seemed my eyes were asking more frankly than my tongue.

The doctor said after a while looking at me, "the condition is rather stable, is he your relative?"

"Yes, very if this will help," I said.

I approached the bed, looked at the face and tried to establish some contact, but the eyes were closed on secrets they might foretell. I touched the hand stretched to my side. The fingers seemed to move interpreting what the eyes hide. The body was reaching its highest subtlety. The secret was still covered by a strong will.

The doctor, observing my deep concern, said after few moments, "we are taking all care, you should not worry too much", and then added, "you better wait outside."

When I reached the waiting area, I found that outside was nowhere. The face was still haunting me with its closed eyes and the touch of hands did not disrupt. The agony was somehow announcing itself, was that the outside meant by the doctor? I did not know why I decided to wait and what for. What could I provide more than the hospital and a good doctor would do?

The time was passing paying no attention to any claim, fair or otherwise. The hospital was very quiet at this moment of night when a strong feeling urged me to his room. A soft light was dispersing through as I slowly opened the door. He was lying on the bed as I saw him a while ago, only the face was directed towards the door, the eyes opened with a look of anticipation.

He smiled when he saw me with sort of relief and said, "thank you for waiting, I didn't expect it, I know you are always busy."

I inquired while approaching the bed seeking his outstretched hand, "how do you feel? I am concerned a bit."

"You are right, now is the best moment to check my body's ability to face its future," he said.

"The doctor is confident of your strength," I encouraged myself.

He smiled in defiant and said, "he seems well informed." Then vaguely added, "at the end of a journey the needs are different, changing course may worry the master, but I don't see many clouds."

I looked at him like a cloud welcoming its future in the wide space, then said, " I wish I could have much of your strength, it is awful to feel helpless".

He ignored my weakness and said, "don't feel sad unless you have a very good reason."

"You still believe in life choices", I said trying to reach him.

He said as a matter of fact, "now only beliefs count, with such clarity who needs a brain"

His eyes closed with content and self-satisfaction, while the hand was still holding mine. Somehow, I felt my agony. It seemed he also felt it because he asked me to come closer so his other hand can reach my shoulder. When it rested there, he said, "will is faster than wisdom, don't reject what your hands have done, they are part of your choice. It is easier that way."

I felt the hand on my shoulder tenderly shaking me. I opened my eyes to find the nurse standing by my side waiting till I woke up and then said, "the doctor wants to see you in the room". She referred to the same room.

When I entered, the doctor was facing the door. The white linen to the face covered the man on bed. The doctor looked at me and said, "you may have your farewell look."

I uncovered the face enough for my eyes to say goodbye. The face had the same satisfaction, a smile I could trace on the lips. I didn't know how long I kept looking at him for the doctor took me by the arm outside the room and said with nonprofessional emotion, "too much sorrow could break your heart"

I heard myself saying, "but I hardly can feel such sorrow, could there be feelings not yet known to us?"

The doctor became more professional while saying, "sorrow may have several meanings and effects, I wish you self-solace."

On my way, back home, the streets were empty, who would care for a lonely passer in the heart of a night. Expectations and possibilities had mixed up with limitations and frustrations. I stopped by the sea and waited long enough for the day to break. The darkness seemed so dense beyond penetration, but I was sure of its pregnancy. It was not before long when the first signs of day birth announced themselves. That was not very difficult. Following the sun slowly rising, I asked myself, "is there ever a very good reason to feel sad?"

14. Most unwelcome

His travels are always within places and through times. His message is to be wherever and whenever. Difficulties as hard as could be never stopped him trying again and again. Nobody can deny him being around at a time. He never fails a man who really called for him. He cares for every human. He has this unlimited power and unspecified capacity.

He had heard about a new founded place at the far end of the earth in the middle of a time, and had decided to travel there, continuing his everlasting existence. The place was well known but the way to reach it was too exhaustive. As usual he was prepared to pay all necessary sacrifices, so he persistently started the journey. Every time he stopped to check his whereabouts, he received the same answer, which was "the place is still farther". He knows that a place is easily reached for a welcomed traveler. So, this place was only promising more challenge.

One of the people was curious to ask him "why you insist to travel to this far place? The weather there does not suit health like yours, if you excuse me, Sir."

He smiled to him and said, "I am not as old as I may look, and travel has always been a destiny".

One early morning he woke up to surprisingly find the most magnificent city a man could dream of, just in front of him. The buildings were so greatly built and decorated with colorful artefacts; he had never seen before. There was a special scent flowing from the city capable to turn any head, as if this city was the most beautiful woman clothed, painted and perfumed as richly as imaginable. But then there was a wall around the city and an entrance gate. There was a control of whom to goes in or comes out. For a while he noticed that it was a heavily restricted control. The guards were very alert expecting some intruder.

He approached the gate with natural confidence and started his first step in when he heard the guards 'voice stopping him for checking, "please Sir, may I get your attention for a moment please."

"Surely, my attention is total and permanent," he said while getting closer to the guard.

"It is your first visit to the city, isn't it?" the guard asked.

"I came immediately when I heard about y-our city", he hesitantly answered.

"You came from a very far place, it seems", the guard said.

"But still in the present, you are not history yet", he said. "I am not a late arrival, am I?" then he added.

"Arrival you sure are, late or not I can't judge. We need to know who you are and why", insisted the guard.

"What do you mean by who, is it my name or my real being? Why is too relevant", he inquired.

"It makes no difference to us, just answer the question", the guard responded.

"It makes also no difference to me. Will you let me in afterwards or I might be hindered all the same?" he wondered.

The guard smiled coldly and said, "It makes a difference in this case, now what?"

"May I ask you first about the name of this strange place, or the real being," he asked the guard.

"How did you travel to a place you did not know its name or the being of it?"

"It is part of my real being my friend. And, the name they gave me is Conscience."

The guard's features suddenly changed, his face became so rigid and severe. With a very fast move he closed the gate to keep the man outside his city and said when he ensured his task, "and the name of this city, Sir, is Technology, part of its real being is not to permit you an entry."

15. The Candles Village

You notice the sign of "The Candles Village" as you approach Alexandria from Cairo desert road, something like 40 kilometers away.

"It is one of the oldest villages in the Nile Delta that goes back deep in time, thousands of years" my bus neighbor and narrator tried to impress me.

His eyes were fixed on the sign as the bus was speeding up its way towards Alexandria. There was nothing to impress anybody though, with the dust filling the air and the chaos that enveloped the two-way road, except probably the admiration and pride in the narrator's eyes while the words flowing from his mouth. I did not recall asking him what was behind his sudden attention on the sign, but he volunteered to tell me nevertheless.

"That is the first village to produce candles in Egypt. That goes back thousands of years when old Egyptian extracted the tallow from cattle and sheep and used it to make their wicked candles before Romans did it."

I closed the book I was reading and, to be polite, I showed him some interest.

"Can you believe that every house of this village was making candles continuously day and night?" he continued.

He did not wait for my answer and just carried on, "the night in this village was lighted like a sunny day hence all their days were sunny. The darkness was never there, transparency dominated the life of the villagers and they provided the source of light to other villages too".

I tried to interrupt him with a note of surprise or disbelief but he did not stop to allow me a word and continued: "generation after generation continued to make candles. Everyone was holding a candle wherever he or she goes day and night. There was no secret between the villagers or a place to hide one".

"They needed night to sleep like all sane people", I managed to comment on his unbelievable story.

"My friend, you don't need darkness to be sane or a secret to be human", he sounded completely convinced of what he was saying.

"Is that still the case till now?" I asked him to try not to show my sarcasm.

He did not indicate any expression of being ridiculed. Ignoring my question, he said,

" that was the case until that day when a stranger visited the village..."

He stopped reflecting for some moments as if a sad memory crossed his mind, then continued, giving me the feeling that he does not care whether I am interested by his story telling or not,

"In the beginning no one paid him a special attention imagining he is one of the everyday many comers seeking to buy the famous candles of the village. But then his questions – like yours- attracted the attention of many of the villagers crossed his way."

Suddenly I felt myself curious and my ears became attentive to follow his story which he was telling no one, but himself. "What kind of questions can make people living in a continuous light so curious?" I asked.

"My friend, that is exactly what he questioned. He asked them: how could you sleep if there is no night? What is your magic that made your day endless? Everyone provided the same reply surprised of the question and who is asking"

"What was the answer" I could not help my impatience to ask.

"They just told him that they know only one thing; which is how to make candles and nothing else".

I kept my silence awaiting him to explain a bit more, but he kept silent also for a long time until he sensed me staring at him. Then he said with a deep breath, "That was the end of the village's legend. The stranger showed them how to create darkness and have nights"

When he recognized the look in my eyes as an accusation of him being insane, he added, "With the darkness, secrets found the way to their world, lies could be protected, and the demand for candles became less and less. After a little while the village became like all other villages; having only some light sufficient to see each other, and darkness thick enough for everyone to hide himself from the others and even from oneself. The days were not as sunny as they used to be, and permitted the nights to exist. There were not enough candles. After that, the stranger left. The village lost its entity, only its name remained. I probably am the last one who still recalls its history"

"I never heard of this episode and find it hard to believe", I said, not caring of his possible anger.

"You are not the first one not to believe my story, no one believed it, but I will keep telling it because it is the true story of this village, everyone has the right to know it. Don't believe any other story". He said that and stood up to leave the bus although it did not reach its destination yet. He did not bid me farewell either. He was completely lost in his world.

My frequent trips to Alexandria through the desert road were never the same after that day. I always locate the sign of the Candles Village and think about that story and its teller.

Zeitfracht Medien GmbH
Ferdinand-Jühlke-Straße 7
99095 Erfurt, Deutschland
produktsicherheit@kolibri360.de